RUDI'S POND

by EVE BUNTING

illustrated by
RONALD HIMLER

CLARION BOOKS • NEW YORK

Clarion Books
a Houghton Mifflin Company imprint
215 Park Avenue South, New York, NY 10003
Text copyright © 1999 by Eve Bunting
Illustrations copyright © 1999 by Ronald Himler

First Clarion paperback edition, 2004.

The illustrations were executed in watercolor.
The text was set in 16-point Weiss.

www.houghtonmifflinbooks.com

Printed in China

Library of Congress Cataloging-in-Publication Data

Bunting, Eve, 1928–
Rudi's pond / by Eve Bunting ; illustrated by Ronald Himler.
p.   cm.
Summary: When a sick boy dies, his friends and classmates remember him by building
a schoolyard pond in his memory.
ISBN 0-395-89067-5
[1. Death—Fiction. 2. Friendship—Fiction.] I. Himler, Ronald, ill. II. Title.
PZ7.B91527Ru   1999   98-51338
[E]—dc21   CIP   AC

CL ISBN–13: 978-0-395-89067-7   CL ISBN–10: 0-395-89067-5

PA ISBN–13: 978-0-618-48604-5   PA ISBN–10: 0-618-48604-6

LEO 10 9 8 7 6 5 4
4500341649

If I were a hummingbird

I would get nectar for you,

and I would help flowers grow

for you.

—*Tobin*
Diana's kindergarten class

Rudi and I lived on the same street. So he was my friend at school and at home, too.

Rudi didn't mind having play tea parties with me.
He liked my dolls.

We went on nature hikes with my uncles and aunts
and my cousins. We knew a pond and we'd go there and
put our feet in the water. One time we saw an egret.
But Rudi was sick a lot and sometimes he couldn't come
with us. Still, we did a lot of things together.

Our garden gate is green and one day we painted it
all over with yellow tulips. We made it so beautiful.

One Saturday we made a hummingbird feeder
from a bottle and a drinking straw. We cut out
cardboard petals and stuck them to the straw so
it looked like a flower.

"They'll come for sure," Rudi said. "It's such a great-
looking feeder. If I was a bird, I'd come. We just have
to wait."

When Rudi was sick, I'd go to his house after
school. We'd play computer games. Or color.
Rudi was a real good colorer.

Then one day his mom called my mom and said Rudi was sinking and they'd taken him to the hospital.

I didn't understand "sinking."

"It means he's very, very ill," Mom told me.

"But what's the matter with him? Why is he always sick?" I asked.

"When Rudi was born, there was something wrong with his heart. It's been getting worse." Mom held me tight against her.

Rudi was in that hospital for a long time.

We sent cards and our class made a big GET WELL RUDI banner for his hospital room. I asked and asked if I could go visit him. But only his mom and dad were allowed to see him.

"What if we never get to talk again?" I shouted. "He's my best friend. It's not fair!"

Mom stroked my hair. "I know it's not fair, sweetheart. None of this is fair."

I never did get to talk to Rudi again because he died
in that hospital.
   When Mom and Dad told me, we hugged and
hugged and cried. I thought I'd never stop.

They let me stay in their bed that night and they
held my hands, one on each side of me, till I fell asleep.
The next morning it was bad all over again.
"Was it just a horrible dream?" I asked Dad.
"No, sweetie," he said. "I wish it were."

In school we wrote poems about Rudi and stapled them together to make a book. Mine said:

Rudi was my friend
He'll be my friend
For ever and ever.

I drew a hummingbird at the bottom of the page.

The principal said we should make something in memory of Rudi, something lasting.

"Poems last," I said, and everyone agreed. But we needed a memorial that would be a part of the school.

"Maybe a tree," our teacher said.

"Maybe a fountain," the principal suggested.

"He liked ponds," I said.

That was it.

The pond is beside the big knobby oak in the schoolyard that Rudi and I used to climb. It's small and has a cement ring around it. While the cement was wet, we wrote our names in it, so Rudi's pond is in the middle of all of us. We brought rocks and shells to pile around the edges and plants to make it even prettier.

    "Rudi and I made a hummingbird feeder once,"
I told my teacher. "Could I bring it and hang it on
the tree?"

    She said I could.

    My desk in our classroom is by the window,
and I hung the feeder where I could see it.

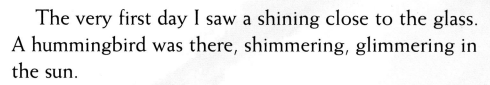

The very first day I saw a shining close to the glass.
A hummingbird was there, shimmering, glimmering in
the sun.
   I was looking at it and it was looking at me.
   My heart thumped.

I watched it flash toward Rudi's pond and drink
from the flower straw. Seeing it there made me
feel so happy.

The same hummingbird came the next day and the next. I could tell it was the same one because it had the same face. Always it came to the window first, to me.

I had the strangest thought, but I knew it couldn't possibly be true. Probably the hummingbird came to see itself in the glass. But the thought I had wouldn't go away. I might tell my mom. It's easy to tell her things.

Soon it will be summer vacation.

I'm taking the feeder home and I'll hang it in our yard. I'll keep it filled with fresh sugar water every day.

I wonder if the hummingbird will be able to find my house. It's the one with the green gate that's painted all over with yellow tulips.

I think the hummingbird will remember.